LULU'S

To Lawy and Jeff…
And Jayley and Xanna…
Lulu would be proud of you all!
Love from Mom and Aunt Beta

—E. F. H.

For Otto

—P. C.

Lulu's Birthday
Text copyright © 2001 by Elizabeth Fitzgerald Howard
Illustrations copyright © 2001 by Pat Cummings
All rights reserved.
Printed in Hong Kong by South China Printing Company (1988) Ltd.
www.harperchildrens.com

Watercolors, gouache and colored pencils
were used for the full-color art.
The text type is Perpetua.

Library of Congress Cataloging-in-Publication Data

Howard, Elizabeth Fitzgerald.
Lulu's birthday / by Elizabeth Fitzgerald Howard; pictures by Pat Cummings.
    p.   cm.
"Greenwillow Books."
Summary: Laurie and J. Matthew plan a birthday surprise for Lulu.
Includes a recipe for "One-Two-Three-Four Cake."
ISBN 0-688-15944-3 (trade).   ISBN 0-688-15945-1 (lib. bdg.)
[1. Birthdays—Fiction. 2. Afro-Americans—Fiction.]
I. Cummings, Pat, ill.   II. Title.   PZ7.H83273Lu 2001
[E]—dc21   98-032206

1 2 3 4 5 6 7 8 9 10   First Edition

BIRTHDAY

By Elizabeth Fitzgerald Howard

Pictures by Pat Cummings

GREENWILLOW BOOKS
An Imprint of HarperCollins Publishers

"Children," Lulu said, "summer is flying by,
and soon you will be going home.
But today is my birthday. I want you
to help me celebrate this afternoon.
Let's go back to some special place where
we had a special good time this summer.
Where shall we go?"

Laurie and J. Matthew looked at each
other. Laurie whispered something
to J. Matthew.

Then Laurie said, "Lulu, I have an idea. Remember when we went to the zoo? And we saw seals reaching for rings and tigers wrestling in their water hole? And we had a picnic, too! Can we celebrate your birthday at the zoo?"

"Laurie, that's a splendid idea!" said Lulu. "We'll see seals and tigers and monkeys and elephants and flamingos and crocodiles. And of course we'll have a picnic! Let's celebrate my birthday at the zoo!"

"No, no, Lulu," said J. Matthew. "I have an idea. Remember when we went to the beach? And we made a little village out of sand? And we put small stones for streets and fences, and shiny shells for windows? And then that really big wave came and washed it all away? Can we celebrate your birthday at the beach?"

"The beach!" said Lulu. "Wonderful, J. Matthew! Get your swimsuits! Get your shovels! Let's celebrate my birthday at the beach!"

"No, no, I have an idea, Lulu!" Laurie said. "Remember when we went to the ballet? We sat so high up in the balcony, we thought we might fall out. But we had your opera glasses, so we could see everything—even the sparkly diamonds on the dancers' dresses? Remember, Lulu? Can we celebrate your birthday at the ballet?"

"That's a lovely thought, Laurie!" said Lulu. "We'll take my opera glasses again, so we can watch the dancers wiggling their ears. Let's celebrate my birthday at the ballet!"

"No, no, Lulu!" said J. Matthew. "I have an idea!
Remember when we went to the movies and it was
really fun and scary? And you hugged us so we wouldn't
stay scared? Can we celebrate your birthday at the movies?"

"Oh, J. Matthew, yes. Why not?" said Lulu.
"We'll sit close together and eat lots of popcorn.
Yes, let's celebrate my birthday at the movies!"

"No, no, Lulu!" said Laurie. "Remember the time we were at the baseball game and Buzz and James Harold were with us and I almost caught a fly ball? Can we celebrate your birthday at the baseball game?"

"Oh, Laurie, what a marvelous plan!" said Lulu. "We can sing and shout till our throats are scratchy. Can you find your glove? Let's celebrate my birthday at the baseball game!"

Laurie and J. Matthew looked at each other.

Then Laurie whispered something to J. Matthew.

"Oh, Lulu, we have another idea," said J. Matthew.

"We're going to take YOU somewhere."

"Not the zoo, not the beach, not the ballet," said Laurie.

"Not the movies, not the ball game," said J. Matthew.

"Close your eyes, Lulu," said Laurie.

"Don't peek, Lulu!" J. Matthew said.

"My goodness," said Lulu. "What is happening?"

Laurie and J. Matthew took hold
of Lulu's hands.

"Come this way, Lulu," said Laurie.

They turned a little this way, and
then turned a little that way.

They turned Lulu around
and around in a circle.

"My goodness," said Lulu.
"What is going on?"

They all walked slowly out
the door and onto the porch.

"No fair trying to peek, Lulu,"
said Laurie.

"Sit here, Lulu," said J. Matthew.

"My goodness, this feels
like my own comfy chair,"
said Lulu.

"Now!" shouted
Laurie and J. Matthew.

"SURPRISE!"

Everyone was there. Aunt Flossie
and Uncle Howard. Aunt Emma
and Uncle Alfred. Aunt Erma
and Uncle Brad. Uncle Nelson.
Uncle Will. Cousin Chita.
Cousin Jessie. Cousin Gladys.
Cousin Anne. Buzz and James
Harold from the next house.
Mr. Briscoe from the farm
down the road. And everybody
was singing, "Happy Birthday,
dear Lulu!"

"My goodness!" Lulu said. "How wonderful! You really surprised me! How did you all sneak over here? And who baked this beautiful cake?"

"We made it, Lulu. We made it!" said J. Matthew and Laurie. "We made it at Aunt Flossie's house."

"My goodness," said Lulu. "You are such smart children!"

"Do you like your birthday, Lulu?" Laurie asked.

"Oh, yes!" said Lulu. "This is better than the zoo, better than the beach, better than the ballet, better than the movies, better than the baseball game! It is the best! Thank you for my birthday surprise!"

ONE-TWO-THREE-FOUR CAKE
(Bert Fitzgerald's recipe)

Preheat oven to 350 degrees.
It is best to have the ingredients at room temperature.

YOU WILL NEED

1 cup milk	**4 egg yolks**
1 cup butter	**4 egg whites**
or margarine	**$2\frac{1}{4}$ teaspoons baking powder**
2 cups sugar	**$\frac{1}{4}$ teaspoon salt**
3 cups flour	**$1\frac{1}{2}$ teaspoons vanilla**

- Combine in a medium-sized bowl the flour, baking powder, and salt. Set aside.
- Combine the milk and vanilla. Set aside.
- In a large mixing bowl beat the butter until soft.
- Gradually add the sugar. Beat until light.
- Beat in the 4 egg yolks one by one.
- Beat in one-third of the flour mixture, then one-third of the milk-vanilla
  mixture. Beat until smooth after each addition.
- Repeat until all the flour and all the milk have been combined.
- Whip 4 egg whites until stiff but not dry. Fold them gently into the batter.
- Bake in a greased and floured tube pan for about 45 minutes.
- Try to wait for the frosting before eating it all up!

FROSTING

YOU WILL NEED

2 cups confectioners' sugar	**2 tablespoons milk**
2 tablespoons warm melted butter	**1 teaspoon vanilla**
	Food coloring

- Combine the confectioners' sugar with the melted butter, milk, and vanilla.
- Add the food coloring. Beat until smooth and spreadable.
- If it is too thick, add more milk. If it is too thin, add more sugar.
- Let the cake cool. Then spread the frosting on the top and on the sides.